Walt Disney's
Mickey Mouse
and the
BEST-NEIGHBOR CONTEST

 GOLDEN PRESS
Western Publishing Company, Inc.
Racine, Wisconsin

One midsummer day, Mickey Mouse called all his
friends to a special meeting. Minnie Mouse, Goofy,
and Mickey's nephews, Morty and Ferdie, were there,
along with Donald Duck and *his* nephews.

"Friends," Mickey began, "it's a long, hot summer, and I think we're all in a slump, just like a losing baseball team. We'll have to do something to stir things up."

Minnie Mouse nodded. "You're right, Mickey, but what? Have you any ideas?"

"Yes," he answered. "We'll have a contest!"

Everybody brightened.

"What kind of contest?" Donald Duck asked.

"A best-neighbor contest," Mickey replied. "Each of us must think of something to do to help everybody enjoy summertime. I'll be the judge, and the 'best neighbor' will win a silver loving cup!"

They all started shouting excitedly. "I'll run a pet
show!" Minnie decided, recalling all the different
kinds of pets her friends owned.

"We'll open a lemonade stand!" Morty yelled.

"Right!" agreed Ferdie. "Free ice-cold lemonade
for everybody!"

"I'll get my big balloon ready!" Donald cried. "I'll
give everyone free rides!"

Then Donald's nephews offered their new playground equipment for the children. "They can use our seesaw!" said Huey.

"And our swing!" said Dewey.

"And our slide!" added Louie.

"Those are all *great* ideas," Mickey said. "What about you, Goofy? What's *your* idea for the Best-Neighbor Contest?"

"Shucks, I don't know," Goofy answered, "but I'll try to think of something." With a faraway look in his eyes, he turned and walked off toward his house.

The Best-Neighbor Contest soon opened, and it ran for a whole week. Everybody in town came and then came back, again and again, to enjoy the fun. Mickey made his rounds every day, keeping an eye on things so he could decide fairly who should win the Best-Neighbor prize.

At Minnie's pet show, Goofy was saying hello to a turtle, a skunk, and a hamster when Mickey came along. "Wow, Mickey," Goofy said enviously, "Minnie sure had a swell idea for the contest. I wish I could have thought of something to do for everyone."

At Morty and Ferdie's lemonade stand, Goofy looked wistfully at the row of ice-cold pitchers as he smacked his lips over his own tall glass of the drink. "These kids are being real nice to their neighbors," he said. "Everyone loves lemonade."

Later, at Donald's balloon ride, Mickey watched as Goofy floated across a field in the basket of the balloon and landed gently and safely. "Donald's ride is terrific," Goofy said longingly. "But me? I couldn't come up with a single thing."

At the playground, the neighborhood children were shouting with glee as they seesawed, swung, and slid. Goofy, standing at the bottom of the slide to catch the littlest children as they came down, thought, *Huey, Dewey, and Louie sure have some fun stuff here. Why couldn't I think of anything to do for the Best-Neighbor Contest?*

On Friday night, the contest ended, and on Saturday, Mickey invited all his friends to a hot-dog party on his front lawn.

"I'm going to award the prize for the Best-Neighbor Contest," he announced, "but all of you have been so great, I haven't yet made up my mind who the winner is. First, I want to compliment each of you on your great work.

"Minnie, your pet show went off without a hitch. How did you manage with so many different pets? Not one pet got lost or ran away!"

"That's because Goofy looked after them," Minnie replied. "He was wonderful. He took personal charge of every single pet!"

Mickey turned to Morty and Ferdie. "Boys, I'm proud of all the hard work you did. It must have been a tough job to squeeze all those lemons."

"No," Morty explained, "Goofy came early and did most of the squeezing, just to help us out."

Next, Mickey spoke to Donald Duck. "Donald," he said, "you were pretty clever to fill that balloon with air and keep it filled."

"Don't give *me* the credit," Donald said. "Goofy checked it every day, then pumped every night to keep the balloon filled with air."

Then Mickey spoke to Donald's nephews. "Boys, the way you ran your playground was perfect. Everybody had fun without getting hurt."

"It was Goofy!" exclaimed Huey.

"He kept an eye on the children all day," added Dewey.

"That's why nobody got hurt," said Louie.

Mickey thought for a minute. "Friends," he said finally, "this is really heartwarming. I think you'll all agree that the only one of you who said he couldn't think of an idea has turned out to be the best neighbor of all! I mean Goofy, of course, the one who has helped everyone the most! Goofy wins the silver loving cup!"

Everybody cheered. "Hooray! Goofy is our best neighbor!"

But when they turned to look for the winner, he wasn't there. They searched and finally found him working at the barbecue grill, roasting hot dogs for the whole crowd. "How about that Goofy!" said Mickey. "Even though the contest is over, he's *still* being everybody's best neighbor!"

"Hot dogs, coming up!" called Goofy with a big, neighborly smile.